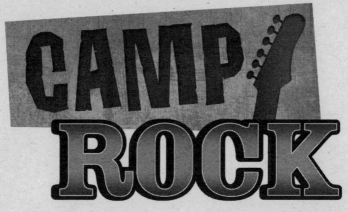

The Junior Novel

Adapted by Lucy Ruggles

Based on "Camp Rock," Written by Karin Gist & Regina Hicks and Julie Brown & Paul Brown

D0104798

New York
An Imprint of Disney Book Group

CHAPTER ONE

"**M**itchie, up!" Connie Torres commanded as she stepped through the piles of clothes and CDs on her fourteen-year-old daughter's bedroom floor. "Last day of school!" She clapped her hands cheerfully before disappearing down the hall.

In the bed, Mitchie stirred and groaned. Her hand shot out from under the covers and grabbed a CD labeled MITCHIE'S TUNES from the nightstand. Without looking, Mitchie popped the disc into the CD player and pushed PLAY.

Instantly, the chords of a pop song filled the

room. It featured vocals by none other than Mitchie Torres herself. As the beat intensified, Mitchie threw off her covers and jumped out of bed. She pulled her long, brown hair back, and singing the words she knew by heart, she opened her closet and peered in.

What to wear? The jean miniskirt? She held it up to her hips. Nope. The skirt was looking a little too mini. Shorts? Nope. Same problem. Pants, she thought. Maybe? Grabbing a pair of capris from a hanger, she tried them on. Better, but not perfect. Then she spied leggings, and inspiration flared. A skirt, leggings, a T-shirt— the perfect, not-too-dressy, last-day-of-school outfit.

In the middle of putting on a long necklace, Mitchie was hit with an idea. She hurried from her closet to her desk, where she grabbed a journal. On the front, in bold letters, was written "Mitchie's Songs." She furiously scribbled some lyrics on a blank page. Satisfied with the new verses, Mitchie smiled, put the journal away, and continued dancing out of her room, down the hall, and into the kitchen, where her mother had set out breakfast.

Mitchie plopped down at the kitchen table, and began to scarf down an omelet. On the television, an entertainment show discussed the most recent antics of Shane Gray—musician *and* hottie.

"The pop-star phenomenon, Shane Gray," the television reporter intoned, "may have gone too far this time when he stormed off the set of his new video after someone gave him a grande nonfat latte instead of his legendary Venti soy chai latte with extra foam. This final stunt cost his label thousands of dollars, but may cost *him* his record deal."

Mitchie sighed. Shane Gray had everything. Why would he want to ruin it?

"The message is clear," the reporter went on. "He needs to clean up his act. And to give him time to do it, the Connect Three summer tour has been canceled."

The report was almost over when Mitchie's mother sat down in the seat next to her.

"Look what I found in the crisper," Connie said, tossing a colorful, glossy booklet onto the table. "A Camp Rock brochure. Or should I say *another* Camp Rock brochure?" she added.

"Hmm, look at that!" Mitchie said, faking surprise. She shoveled another forkload of omelet into her mouth. So maybe the hints she'd been dropping about going to Camp Rock this summer hadn't been as subtle as she thought. But if she got in, all her dreams could come true.

"So, you have no knowledge of how this brochure got into the refrigerator?" her mother asked. "Or the one taped to the vacuum cleaner?"

Mitchie shrugged.

"Sweetie," Connie continued, "I know you want to go to this camp, but we just can't swing it right now with Dad expanding the store and my catering business just taking off, and . . . I'm sorry," she said gently.

Mitchie's mood deflated. Deep down she had figured Camp Rock was out of the question, but a girl could hope. . . .

4

"I know," she said, standing to take her empty plate to the sink. "Well, gotta go. Last day of school. Don't want to be late."

The halls were abuzz with last-day-of-school energy. Students were joking with each other as they joyfully dumped old notebooks, tests, and quizzes into the overflowing garbage cans.

Mitchie opened her locker to find a year's worth of clutter—crumpled papers, worn-out pencils, leaky pens, and textbooks—jammed in at odd angles.

She sighed and began throwing various items into the trash. A Camp Rock brochure caught her eye. She sighed and tossed it into the trash, too.

She was still cleaning a few minutes later when Sierra, a lanky girl with glasses, walked up and opened the locker next to Mitchie's. Sierra was Mitchie's best friend—her only friend.

"Let me be the first to say *xin xia ji*!" Sierra exclaimed, acknowledging summer's arrival. "Guess who got an A-plus in AP Mandarin? *Me*. Again!"

Sierra screamed excitedly, but Mitchie didn't feel like joining in the celebration of her friend's achievement just now. She was too distracted by a group of popular girls floating down the hall.

"Ugh," Sierra groaned. "The Queen Bees are here. If we don't move, they won't sting." She rolled her eyes, but Mitchie watched the girls enviously.

"Don't you ever wonder what it would be like to be one of them?" Mitchie asked.

Sierra gave her friend a suspicious look. "Are you feeling feverish?" She jokingly put her hand on Mitchie's forehead. "So," she said, changing the subject, "how'd it go this morning?"

"It didn't," Mitchie said dejectedly. "Camp Rock is a no-go."

"But you *have* to go! Camp Rock is, like, *the* music camp. Everybody who wants to be some-body in music—" Sierra stopped when she saw the unhappy look on Mitchie's face. "—All of which you already know. Sorry."

Mitchie swept the remaining junk from her

locker into the trash and closed the door one last time. "Me, too. I was so excited to go and have a summer that's all about music."

Sierra closed her own locker and put a hand consolingly on Mitchie's shoulder. Then she asked the only thing she could. "So, what *are* you going to do this summer?"

CHAPTER TWO

Unfortunately, Mitchie's dreams of a rock-filled summer were replaced with the harsh reality of waiting tables. Not the glamorous break she had imagined, but it would keep her busy and hopefully earn her some cash.

She was still bummed, however, when she got home the evening after her first shift. The smell of burgers wafted through the house. Following the scent, Mitchie walked into the backyard. Her mother greeted her with a plastic plate holding a large, juicy hamburger.

"Our world-famous Torres burger!" Connie declared.

Mitchie's father, Steve, waved from his spot manning the grill.

"Uh . . . I'll pass," Mitchie said, feeling slightly nauseous. She had seen enough hamburgers for one day.

"Okay," her father said, his eyes twinkling despite the sad expression on his daughter's face. "I can't stand it. Tell her."

"Tell me what?" Mitchie asked, confused.

Her mother's face broke into a wide smile. "You're going to Camp Rock!" she cried.

Mitchie's mouth fell open as she stared at her parents in disbelief.

"Actually," corrected her mother, grinning as she sat down at the picnic table, "*we're* going. Connie's Catering is going camping."

As the words sank in, Mitchie let out a loud shriek and began jumping up and down.

Connie unfolded her napkin in her lap as her daughter continued to celebrate. "Business is slow in the summer," she explained. "This is a steady job, and you get to go to camp for a discounted rate. But you have to help out in the kitchen."

Mitchie didn't care. She would clean the bathroom, too, if they asked. "Thank you," Mitchie said, wrapping her arms around her mother and then her father. "Thank you, like, a million times!"

"I think she's excited," her father said, shooting a wink at his wife.

Connie nodded, and Mitchie beamed as she squeezed them tighter. She was going to Camp Rock!

CHAPTER THREE

Mitchie's eyes were wide as she took in the scene passing outside the car window. Her mother steered their van by a huge sign at the camp entrance that read, CAMP ROCK. Once on the grounds, Mitchie saw SUVs and tiny sports cars pulled up in front of the check-in area. Rustic cabins dotted the campgrounds.

Campers and counselors roamed around. They had name tags resembling backstage passes dangling from their necks. From what

Mitchie could see, it looked as if the campers had already started to form groups: the goths had found each other, the hip-hoppers, the emos, the angry-chick music girls, the heavy-metal heads, the country crooners, and, of course, the rockers. One group had pulled out sheet music and was singing a cappella. Another was jamming intently on their instruments.

"Excited?" Connie asked.

"A little . . . okay, a lot," Mitchie conceded. "Major. Yes, yes! Thanks, Mom!" she gushed. "I'm gonna have so much—"

Mitchie's attention was stolen midsentence by a girl stepping out of a white stretch limo. The light caught the girl's long, blonde hair as she gabbed on her rhinestone-encrusted cell phone. Two assistants dutifully unloaded her designer luggage from the trunk of the limo.

Mitchie's mouth dropped. So that's what the Queen Bee of Camp Rock looked like. Before she could get a closer look, Connie drove the van behind the mess hall.

One thing was clear—this was going to be a very interesting summer.

"**A**nd then my mom got me backstage passes to Shane's concert," Tess, the Queen Bee that Mitchie had just spotted, said rather casually into her cell phone. Ella and Peggy, speaking to Tess on their cell phones, fell into step beside her. The two girls made up Tess's entourage. Wherever she went, they followed.

"Too bad they canceled the concert," Peggy said, still speaking on the phone even though Tess was less than a foot away.

"Whatev," Tess answered. "I'm sure he's invited to my mom's big record party next month."

"Your life? Perfect." Ella observed with a shade of envy.

Tess's life did seem pretty perfect. She was rock royalty. Her mother, T.J. Tyler, had topped the charts more times than Tess could remember. There was even a special "Grammy room" in their house just for T.J.'s music awards.

"Yeah, but whatev." Tess sighed into the phone. Before she could go on, she spied a group of girls singing last year's hit song, backed by three guys beat-boxing. She stopped in her tracks. "Wannabes," she scoffed as she closed her phone with a sharp *snap*.

Peggy shut her phone also. "Yeah," she agreed. Then, "Wait, aren't we?"

Tess glared at her. "No. Because this year, *we're* going to win Final Jam," she said confidently.

"That will be so awesome," Ella gushed, her cell phone still attached to her ear.

Tess and Peggy looked at each other and then at their friend. "Uh, Ella," Tess said with a smirk, "we're off the phone."

"Oh, yeah," Ella replied, still into the phone. "Call me back."

Tess and Peggy rolled their eyes. Ella wasn't the sharpest tool in the shed, but she knew how to sing backup vocals.

The cabin Mitchie and her mom would be bunking in was quaint though bare. Sunlight streamed in through the screened windows and onto the twin beds. Mitchie threw her duffel bag on the bed closest to the door and turned toward her mom. "Settled," she said quickly.

But instead of her mom, a man responded from outside. "That's great," the voice said.

Curious, Mitchie and Connie watched as an aging rocker with short hair, faded jeans, and a worn T-shirt entered the cabin.

"Brown Cesario," the man said, extending a hand. "Camp director slash founding member and bass guitar of the Wet Crows. You must be Connie Torres, our new cook."

"That's me," Connie said, shaking his hand. "And this is my daughter—" She turned to introduce Mitchie, but her daughter, and summer kitchen assistant, had slipped out. "—Who is already gone!"

Brown laughed. "She probably just wanted to get out there and get to it. When the music calls, you gotta answer."

"You should meet her," Connie said, laughing

at Brown's assessment. "She's got a *great* voice. Oh, I'm bragging!"

"Gotta brag," said Brown. "Learned that from the Mickster."

Connie looked impressed.

"Backed him up for years on the bass guitar! Great times, but not as great as the time I toured with . . ."

Connie nodded politely. She had a feeling she wasn't going to be able to start dinner for a while—not with Brown in the middle of a story.

CHAPTER FOUR

The campers were gathered in a sunken, stadium-style area for their official Camp Rock welcome. As they waited, a boy named Andy began to bang out a rhythm on the bench with his drumsticks. One by one, the other campers joined in, adding to the beat and dancing and singing.

Mitchie, who had just arrived, watched in awe. She had never seen so much talent gathered in one place! Not looking where she was going, she accidentally bumped into Tess.

17

"Sorry," Mitchie started. "I didn't see you."

"Obviously," Tess snapped and continued walking.

Mitchie stared after her in shock. Talk about rude!

"That's Tess Tyler," explained a girl sitting nearby. "The diva of Camp Rock."

"Is she really good?" Mitchie asked, watching Tess sashay over to an empty seat and sit down as if it were a throne.

"She's good at trying too hard to be good," the girl replied. "Understandable, since her mom is T.J. Tyler."

"*The* T.J. Tyler?" Mitchie's eyes widened in amazement as she turned to look at the girl. "She's got, like, a trillion Grammys."

"A trillion and one, I think. Hi, I'm Caitlyn. Camper today, top-selling music producer tomorrow." She clicked a few buttons on the laptop resting on her knees, and music poured from the speakers. "Check me out."

"Cool. I'm Mitchie."

They were interrupted by the sound of

someone tapping on a microphone. Camp Rock's peppy music director had taken the stage. Everyone fell silent.

"Hi, gang!" she said cheerily. "I'm Dee La Duke."

"Hi, Dee," the crowd chimed, slightly less enthusiastically.

"Uh-huh. Here at Camp Rock, we *SIIIING*!" Dee hit a high note. "So let's hear that again," she said, cupping her hand to her ear.

"Hiii, Deee," the campers sang, imitating her.

Dee grinned, pleased. "Sounds good. A little pitchy in places, but we'll fix that before Final Jam."

Dee's reference to Camp Rock's huge, last-night singing competition brought cheers from the campers. Barron James, a fifteen year old with a reputation for mischief, and Sander Loya, his best friend and partner in crime started an impromptu jam.

Dee smiled from the stage, excited at the kids' enthusiasm. "Okay," she said, quieting everyone again. "This summer isn't all about Final Jam. We've got a lot of work to do. You are going to leave this camp with new music skills. You are going to find your sound and create your own style, figure out who you want to be as an artist, but overall, *HAVE FUN!*" Taking a deep breath, she added, "And . . . drumroll, please."

Andy the drummer started tapping on the stage with his sticks. Dee cleared her throat and looked at him sideways. He stopped.

"For the first time," she continued, "we're going to be joined during camp by a very special celebrity instructor. . . ."

At that moment, the "special" celebrity instructor was getting a surprise of his own.

"I don't want to waste my summer at some camp!" Shane Gray barked at Nate and Jason, the other members of his band, Connect Three.

Shane was, no doubt, a bona fide pop star. But he also had a growing chip on his shoulder. He'd learned the hard way that with fame came pressure. He barely noticed the beauty of the rolling landscape outside the tinted windows of his limo.

"Hey, we used to love that place!" Nate argued. Nate was the leader of the group, a position he was not relishing at that moment. "Three years ago, we were campers."

"Yeah, man, it's where Connect Three . . . connected," piped up Jason in his usual laid-back voice.

Shane still wasn't buying it, so Nate tried a different approach. "You get to see your Uncle Brown."

"Uh, not a selling point," Shane shot back.

Nate understood that his bandmate wasn't thrilled, but he had had enough. "Look, man, you're the bad boy in the press, and the label has a problem with that. Which means, we have a problem with that." When Shane didn't say anything, Nate went on. "This camp thing is supposed to fix that. So do your time. Enjoy the fresh air. Get a tan." He laughed at his own joke as the limo came to a stop.

21

"Ooh, and make me a birdhouse or some-thing," Jason added.

Shane shot him an icy glare. "One word: payback."

"Hey, that's two words," Jason mistakenly pointed out as Shane grabbed the duffel at his feet and opened the door. Still fuming, Shane got out and slammed it behind him.

A moment later the window rolled down and Nate's head popped out. "By the way," he said, a smile tugging at his lips. "We told the press you'd be recording a duet with the winner of Final Jam." With a laugh, the window rolled up and the limo drove away. Shane was stuck at Camp Rock.

Mitchie stared at the large mound of cold, sticky ground beef on the kitchen counter. A stack of hamburger patties was already piled high before her. She sighed and tore off another hunk of meat.

"I hear there's an open mike tonight," her mom said, diligently peeling potatoes beside her.

22

"Yeah," Mitchie confirmed, glumly patting the beef between her palms.

"Are you going to sing?" she pressed.

Mitchie raised an eyebrow. "In front of all those people? No way!"

"Sweetie, I hear you in your room. You're really good." She held up two fingers in the Boy Scout salute. "Mom's honor. You gotta believe in yourself. And if you are nervous, so what? Everyone is nervous." When Mitchie didn't respond, her mother went on. "That's why I'm making so much food tonight. People eat when they're nervous."

Mitchie looked queasily at the pile of raw meat. "Not me. I don't think I can eat another burger. Ever."

Her mother took the half-made hamburger from Mitchie's hands. "Why don't you take the trash to the Dumpster and then set up in the mess hall?"

Mitchie smiled thankfully, wiped her hands on her dirty apron, and swung the ripe garbage bags over her shoulder. She was halfway down the path to the garbage bins when she heard singing. The voice was loud and coming from one of the cabins. Her curiosity getting the better of her, Mitchie tiptoed to the cabin and pressed her nose to the window screen.

Inside, Tess was belting out a song at the top of her lungs. It was good, but Mitchie couldn't help thinking it was overdone. Caitlyn had been right; Tess was trying too hard. Behind her, Peggy and Ella threw in a few "ooohs" and "ahhhs." Suddenly, Tess stopped singing.

"Work with me here, people!" She sighed in exasperation.

Peggy put her hand on her hip. "*Hello!* We're trying. But you're just so—"

Tess glared at her. "Excuse me. I am the one with the Grammys. Well, my mom is." She tried to glide over that little fact. "But she mentioned me in her acceptance speech. If we want to rock tonight at open-mike night, you guys have to listen to me. Let's go again." Tess failed to mention the other reason she was pushing her backup singers—Shane Gray. Ever since Dee had mentioned he was going to be a guest counselor, Tess had been determined to get his attention. And open mike was her first chance.

Outside, Mitchie, realizing how bad it would look if someone saw her, started to back away from the window and tripped on a rock. She fell to the ground, ripping one of the garbage bags and spilling trash everywhere.

"Great," she whispered and struggled to her feet. That was going to leave a bruise.

Across camp, Shane had his cell phone glued to his ear.

"Come on, guys!" he pleaded to his bandmates. "I learned my lesson. I showered in cold water. I looked at a tree. It's been eight hours. I need hair product."

On the other end of the line, Nate stifled a snort. "I guess it's time to embrace the natural look," he joked. Then he hung up on Shane.

Grumbling, Shane shoved the phone into his pocket. When he looked up, he found a pack of screaming girls headed straight for him.

"There he is!" the girls screeched, practically tearing their hair out. *"Shane! Shane!"*

"Great," he muttered. They'd found him. . . .

The Music Mess Hall of Fame looked like any camp cafeteria, except for the signed guitars, old concert posters, and rock T-shirts tacked to the walls.

At the end of the long room, a makeshift stage had been erected. A banner above it read, OPENING NIGHT JAM. Mitchie placed the last set of utensils on the table, and then paused. Glancing around to make sure no one was looking, she climbed onstage. She stood, dreamily imagining an adoring audience hanging on her every note. Pulling out her journal, which was in her apron, she began to sing. Nervously at first, then with confidence, her voice filled the room. It was a song about being more than what everyone sees, about finding your voice even when you're afraid. As she sang, Mitchie forgot where she was. Her voice rose higher and higher.

Outside, Shane was fleeing the pack of crazed

fans. He quickly ducked behind some bushes beside the mess hall as the girls ran screaming past him. Relieved, he sat back and sighed.

Was that someone singing inside? He cocked his head to listen. It was. Shane closed his eyes so he could concentrate on the lyrics. They were good—really good! And so was whomever was singing them.

When the coast was clear, Shane emerged from the bushes and swung through the mess hall's screen door. "Hello?" he called out. "Who's in here?"

But the stage was empty.

CHAPTER FIVE

Inside her cabin, Mitchie rifled madly through her duffel bag while her mother looked on in amusement.

"I've got all the food set up," Connie said, trying not to smile. "So you, princess, are free."

"Gotta find something to wear first," Mitchie said as she dug through her wrinkled T-shirts and jeans.

"Honey, it's camp, not a fashion show."

Mitchie stopped and looked at her mom. "Have you seen these kids? My usual is not going to cut it."

Connie's brow furrowed. "I think you're cute. In a non-mom way. Totally."

Mitchie ignored her and pulled out a simple shirt. "This," she said, holding it up. "This is safe."

"It's also mine," her mother answered. "Honey," she urged, "wear your clothes. Be yourself. You'll be fine."

Mitchie gave her a look, then pulled the shirt over her head.

The open-mike night was going strong as Mitchie watched quietly from the back. She had belted her mom's shirt and was actually pleased with her outfit, but that hadn't helped her confidence. She was nervously tapping her foot to the bass when Caitlyn walked over. A pretty girl with obvious stage presence was beside her.

"Hey," Mitchie said.

"Hey," Caitlyn said with a smile. Nodding at the girl next to her, she added, "This is Lola. Lola, Mitchie."

The three girls chatted for a few moments.

Then Dee announced the next performer—Lola Scott. Smiling, Lola said good-bye and took the stage. A moment later, her voice had captured everyone's attention.

"Wow!" Mitchie gasped. "She's amazing."

"Yeah," Caitlyn agreed. "She should be. Her mom's on Broadway."

"Broadway? Wow."

Caitlyn nodded and leaned back against the wall. "But the kids around here don't care about that. It's all about the bling. That's why Tess runs this camp."

Mitchie looked over at Tess and they made eye contact. Tess and her posse started to walk over.

"Great." Caitlyn rolled her eyes. "Something wicked this way comes."

"Hey, Caitlyn," Tess said with a smirk, sidling up to them, "your folks still wowing 'em on the cruise ships?"

Ella and Peggy laughed.

"Actually, they work in—" Caitlyn began to defend her family, but Mitchie cut her off.

"Hi, I'm Mitchie," she said.

Tess turned and eyed Mitchie. "Oh. Hi," she replied. "I'm Tess Tyler."

"I know. I love your mom," Mitchie gushed. So much for playing it cool on her first night at camp. Beside her, Caitlyn held back a groan as she stepped out of earshot. Apparently, she couldn't watch—or hear—this.

"Of course you do," Tess said, her lips curling in a smile.

"I'm Mitchie Torres." Inwardly, Mitchie groaned. Why had she introduced herself *again*?

Peggy brightened. "Hey, is your dad Nicky Torres, the composer? My dad staged one of his shows."

Suddenly, Tess was more interested. "Is he?"

Mitchie squirmed. "No."

"Oh," Tess replied curtly.

"So what does he do?" Ella asked, smacking her gum.

"He owns a hardware store," Mitchie answered softly.

31

"Let's go," Tess said to Peggy and Ella. After all, without any connections, Mitchie wasn't really worth talking to, Tess thought.

In that split second, Mitchie made a decision. This summer, she could be whomever she wanted to be . . . even a Queen Bee. "But my mom . . ." she started.

"Yes?" Tess said skeptically, half-turning to face her again.

"She's, uh . . . the president of Hot Tunes TV . . . uh, in China. Huge market there." As soon as the words were out of her mouth, she wanted to take them back. But it was too late.

"Wow. Cool," said Tess, completely turning to Mitchie now.

"So cool," Ella chimed in.

"Major cool." Peggy nodded.

Tess looked between Peggy and Ella. "Are you guys thinking what I'm thinking?" she asked.

"Absolutely." Both girls nodded eagerly. There was a pause, then Ella asked, "Wait. What are we thinking?"

Tess rolled her eyes at Ella and turned to Mitchie. "There's an extra bed in our cabin. It's yours if you want it."

"Really?" Mitchie asked, delighted at her change of fortune.

"Totally. We're going to be great friends. Come on, sit with us in the VIP section." Tess grabbed Mitchie by the arm and dragged her off, leaving Caitlyn behind.

"I'm good," Caitlyn said sarcastically as she watched the new "friends" walk away. "Thanks for asking."

Connie was poring through one of the cookbooks stacked on her bed, when Mitchie returned to the cabin after dinner.

"Can you believe," her mother said, without looking up, "not one of these cookbooks has a recipe for chili for three hundred?" She took off her glasses and frowned.

"You don't need a recipe," Mitchie said happily. "Everyone loves your food. It's official."

"Really?" Connie smiled.

"Camper's honor," Mitchie replied.

"So how was open mike? Did you sing?"

"No . . . but I met some girls," Mitchie said cautiously.

Her mother brightened.

"And," Mitchie began, trying not to sound guilty. "They want me to move into their cabin. I know I have to help in the kitchen, but I'll just get up earlier, meet you here, and . . ."

"Sweetie," her mom said with a smile, "of course you can move to the cabin. It'll be fine. Now, I'd better get back to these cookbooks. I've got a rep to protect."

Tess bit her manicured fingernails as she paced the Vibe Cabin and waited on hold on her cell phone. On her bed, Peggy strummed her guitar absently while Ella worked on something equally important—her nails.

"You guys, which color?" Ella asked, holding up two bottles of pink polish.

Peggy, who had stopped plucking her guitar

at Tess's insistence, looked up. "Ella, they are exactly the same."

"So you see my dilemma?" Ella said in earnest.

Suddenly Tess perked up and stopped pacing. "Mom, hey! . . . Yes, I'm totally settled in. Guess what? Shane Gray is . . ." Her face fell. "Yeah, you can totally call me back. Love you, too. Have a good concert."

Tess hung up and for a moment looked as if she might burst into tears. That, or throw her phone across the room. "As usual," she muttered under her breath.

"What, Tess?" Ella asked, pausing over a nail.

Instead of explaining, Tess changed the subject. "My mom says maybe she can get us primo tix to her next concert."

Ella and Peggy clapped at the news just as Mitchie entered the cabin, her duffel bag and guitar case slung over her shoulders. "Hey, guys!" she called, slightly out of breath from the walk over. "Which bed is mine?"

Tess pointed to Peggy's. There was no arguing. Peggy would be moving.

Mitchie plopped her bag on the bed and started to unpack.

Tess peered over her shoulder. "One bag? You can't possibly have all your clothes in there."

"Uh . . . right." Mitchie panicked. "Well, I threw a lot of my clothes away."

Mitchie turned to find Tess going through her duffel bag. She held up one of Mitchie's old, holey T-shirts. "And you kept this?" Tess asked.

"Uh, yeah," Mitchie replied. "It came from China. A little boutique called . . . *Xin Xia Ji*." Thank goodness for Sierra's Mandarin skills, she thought.

"Wow," Peggy said, admiring the shirt. Then, "What does that mean?"

"'Happy summer,'" Mitchie said. "The store is the bomb." Mitchie was eager to bring the subject back to Tess. "Wow, that is a really cool bracelet!"

"It's from my mom," Tess replied, holding up the charm bracelet and admiring how it looked on her wrist. "Every time she wins a Grammy, she adds a charm."

"Totally bling-a-licious," Mitchie said as she continued to unpack. She pulled out her song journal, and then quickly tucked it away.

But Peggy noticed. "Is that your diary?"

Mitchie hesitated before answering. "My songs," she finally explained.

"You write songs?" Tess asked, plopping down on Mitchie's bed.

"Yeah, but they're probably not that good."

"I bet they're good!" Peggy cried. "Let's hear one!"

Mitchie shook her head as Tess grabbed the journal and started flipping through the half-filled pages. "Why not?" Tess asked. "We're friends now, right?"

Mitchie hesitated for a moment. "Well . . . okay," she stammered. Clearing her throat, she started to sing her most recent song, the one she had belted out in the mess hall.

Embarrassed, Mitchie stopped after three verses. "It's not that good," she said, looking away.

Peggy gave Mitchie a look that said she

was crazy. "What? It was totally good. Right, Tess?"

"Totally," Tess agreed in a voice as sweet as a piece of apple pie. Then she tossed the book back to Mitchie—a bit harder than necessary.

CHAPTER
SIX

It was early, and the soft, hazy light of dawn was just beginning to filter through the cracks in the walls of the Vibe Cabin. Outside, it was quiet except for the sounds of chirping birds.

The silence was abruptly pierced by the muffled ring of Mitchie's alarm clock. Mitchie shoved her hand under her pillow to silence the buried clock. She looked around. Ella stirred slightly but fell back to sleep.

The coast clear, Mitchie jumped from her bed, grabbed some clothes, and began to tiptoe past the sleeping girls. Accidentally, her knee bumped Ella's cot.

Ella raised her head, her eyes squinty. "Mitchie?"

"Uh . . . you're dreaming . . . you're a rock princess," Mitchie whispered in a soothing voice.

This pleased Ella, who smiled sleepily. "Okay, I rock," she said before her head dropped heavily back onto her pillow.

Mitchie let out a sigh of relief and made her way out of the cabin and down the path to the kitchen. She had work to do.

A short while later, a line of hungry campers snaked around the mess hall. Slipping out the back unnoticed, Mitchie made her way around to the front, where she joined the impatient throng. Entering the big room, she searched the crowd, looking for a place to sit. She finally spotted an empty seat at a table with Caitlyn, Lola, Barron, and Sander. Catching her eye, Barron waved her over.

"Hey," she said, sliding in next to Caitlyn.

"Slumming, I see?" Caitlyn said.

"What?" Mitchie asked, confused by Caitlyn's cool tone.

At that moment, Tess, Peggy, and Ella came through the mess-hall doors. They spotted Mitchie.

"Hey, Mitchie!" Tess called loudly. "Over here!"

Mitchie glanced over at Caitlyn.

"You'd better go." Caitlyn snickered. "The queen awaits." Then, as Mitchie stood up, Caitlyn asked, "Your music? Are you any good?"

Mitchie didn't know how to answer the question. "I don't know." She shrugged modestly. "Maybe. Kinda."

Caitlyn nodded. "Word of advice," she said. "If you want to be friends with Tess, don't be."

By now, Tess was gesturing and yelling louder at Mitchie from across the mess hall.

"See ya around," Caitlyn said coldly.

Not knowing what to say, Mitchie left. Once at Tess's table, Mitchie immediately got interrogated. "What happened to you this morning?" asked Tess suspiciously.

"Early riser," Mitchie answered quickly. "Yum, toast!" She grabbed a piece of plain toast and stuffed it in her mouth before Tess could ask any more questions.

Meanwhile, someone else's alarm clock had *not* gone off. Shane hadn't even set it. Instead, he was rudely awakened by his uncle ripping off his blankets.

"What the . . . ? What?" Shane grumbled.

"Rise and shine, superstar," Brown said as his nephew groaned and buried his head under the pillow. "Mate, don't make me do this." When Shane made no attempt to get up, Brown picked up a glass of water and threw it on him.

"Hey!" Shane shouted, sitting bolt upright. "I'm up! I'm up!"

"We both have classes to teach," said Brown. "Yours starts in five minutes."

In one of the Camp Rock activity rooms, rows of folding chairs had been set up to face a large piano. Sitting in the front with Tess, Ella, and Peggy, Mitchie couldn't help but feel cool. In another part of the room, Lola and some of her friends were playing around before class, singing and hitting various keys on the piano.

Lola struck one, then became flustered. "Was that a D-flat or a D-sharp?" she asked, looking between her friends.

Tess overheard and leaned over to whisper in Peggy's ear. "She's gotten really good since last year."

Caitlyn, sitting a row behind them, overheard. "What? Are you scared?"

"Of catching your lack of fashion sense?" Tess didn't miss a beat with her insults. "I'm horrified."

Caitlyn smirked and turned away.

"Has anyone actually seen Shane Gray?" Mitchie asked, glancing around at the filled chairs.

"You know," Peggy said, popping a piece of gum in her mouth, "this is the class where he developed his sound."

Mitchie's eyes grew wide. Camp was *so* cool.

Ella, meanwhile, was distracted once again. "Hey, guys, is my lip gloss losing its gloss?"

Impatiently, Andy began beating his desk with his drumsticks. Barron and Sander joined in. They were so caught up in the music that they didn't even notice Brown walk in.

"Whoa," he said, the sound hitting him. "If the class is rockin', I'm glad I came knockin'."

The kids laughed, and everyone settled down.

"So, let's hear what we're working with," Brown said to the rows of campers. "Who wants to sing first? How about . . ." He scanned the room as every single hand went up—except for Mitchie's. "You?"

"Me?" Mitchie asked, glancing behind her.

"Can't argue with the finger," Brown teased.

Mitchie hesitated.

"I'll do it," Tess quickly interjected.

Brown didn't take his eyes off Mitchie. He shook his head. "Nope. The finger picked her."

Mitchie was way uncomfortable now. "Um . . .

okay . . ." she stammered. She stood up and turned to face the room.

"Let 'er rip," Brown said encouragingly. He crossed his arms over his chest and waited.

Mitchie took a beat, and then started to sing very softly.

"I know you're singing a solo," Brown said, "but it's so low, I can't hear you. Louder."

Mitchie nodded and sang louder. Truth be told, she was good, *very* good. Everyone, even Brown, was clearly impressed.

"She's great," Ella whispered to Tess and Peggy.

Tess shot her sidekick a look. She was *not* happy.

"Not bad, not bad," Brown said when Mitchie's song was over. "Is that an original?"

Mitchie felt her cheeks flush as she looked shyly down at her flip-flops. "Yeah. It's mine, but—"

"No buts," Brown countered. "It's good."

Smiling, Mitchie sat back down. Things were definitely off to a great start.

★ ★ ★

"I didn't know you were that good," Peggy said after class. "You totally rocked it!"

"Totally!" Ella agreed, making Mitchie blush.

Tess, who had been oddly quiet since Mitchie's performance, finally spoke up. "So, I've been thinking . . . you have to sing with us in the Final Jam. Your vocals in the background would be like, amazing. We never let people in our group. But you? A must. Want in?"

"Well . . . um . . ." Mitchie stammered. "I was going to sing solo."

"Solo?" Tess asked, feigning shock. "In your first Final Jam? That's brave."

Mitchie gulped. What was Tess getting at? "I'm sure I'll be nervous at first, but—"

"In front of *all* those people," Tess nodded. "Yeah, you'll be fine. I mean, you've done it before." The words were supportive, but the tone was not.

"Done what before?" Mitchie asked, her heart beginning to beat faster.

46

When Tess pointed out that Mitchie would be singing in front of an audience much bigger than one classroom, Mitchie's stomach twisted. "Maybe a group would be better," she said finally.

Tess hid a smile. "If you think so."

Nodding her head, Mitchie tried to sound convincing as she said, "Yeah, it'll be fun."

Just then, Mitchie noticed the time. She was late. "Um, I gotta run," she said, hurrying off in the direction of the mess hall.

"Where?" Tess yelled after her.

"I've got to go call my mom—China time!" Mitchie called over her shoulder. More like china*ware* time, she thought to herself. She was supposed to be setting the tables for dinner.

Connie was hard at work when Mitchie ran through the kitchen door. "Sorry I'm late," she said breathlessly.

"That's okay, honey," her mom said, offering her cheek for a peck. "The last batch of cookies is in the oven. You can start to clean up." She picked up a stack of boxes and headed toward the basement. "I'm going to take these down to the storage room."

Mitchie wiped the counter down with a sponge and grabbed a bag of flour to put back in the lower cabinet. As she bent down, she heard someone enter the kitchen.

"Hello!" a male voice called.

Mitchie's eyes nearly popped out of her head. She couldn't get up! If she did and the voice belonged to a camper, she'd be totally busted! She cowered, hidden behind the counter, and tried to stay silent, but the floor creaked, betraying her.

"Um, hello?" the voice called again.

The floor creaked once more, and Mitchie cringed.

"I can hear you . . ." said the voice.

Panicking, Mitchie grabbed a handful of flour, squinched her eyes shut, and threw the white dust in her face. She held her breath and stood up. And when she saw *who* the voice belonged to—her breath threatened to never return. Shane Gray—*the* Shane Gray—was right there!

"Do you work here?" Shane asked, confused.

Mitchie's stomach clenched. "Yes," she said, resigned to the fact that the jig was up. Everyone would know her mom didn't run Hot Tunes TV China, she ran the kitchen.

Shane raised an eyebrow at her flour-whitened face. "You really get into your work. I'm Shane, but I'm sure even the kitchen help knows that."

Mitchie's stomach unclenched. Shane didn't recognize her! Then again, she thought, it wasn't that big a shock. Unlike him, her face wasn't on the cover of every magazine.

"Of course," she said with a smile. "Nice to meet you."

"Actually," Shane said, sounding annoyed, "it's not so nice. My manager said he sent over my food-allergy list, but since I couldn't go near my breakfast, I'm going to assume your kitchen people didn't get it."

"Excuse me?" Mitchie asked, her tone suddenly icy.

"What?" Shane asked, oblivious to how obnoxious he sounded.

"You're kind of being a jerk," Mitchie said, the butterflies in her stomach replaced with a knot of anger.

"And you are?" Shane replied, his voice filled with attitude.

"A person," Mitchie replied matter-of-factly. "There's a way to talk to a person. And *that's* not it."

Shane was taken aback. No one talked to him like this. He looked at Mitchie a long time—too long for her comfort. She looked away. Luckily, the oven buzzer went off, breaking the tense silence.

"Well, um . . ." Shane stammered, still intrigued by Mitchie's boldness, "I'll have my manager send it over again."

"Fine." Mitchie cleared her throat, waiting for something.

"Thank you?" Shane offered.

"Much better."

Shane left the kitchen, and Mitchie exhaled a sigh of relief, a little puff of white dust coming off her floured face.

She had met Shane Gray—and survived. At least, sort of.

CHAPTER SEVEN

Inside the Vibe Cabin, Tess paced while Ella and Peggy sat cross-legged on their beds, writing letters home.

"We are totally going to win now that Mitchie is singing with us," Ella mused, chewing on the end of her pen.

Tess stopped pacing. "A new *background* singer isn't going to make us win. We need to win Shane over." If he was one of the Final Jam judges and they snagged his vote, there was no way they could lose.

Her thoughts were interrupted by Dee's entrance into the cabin. "Mail time, girls!" the counselor chimed brightly. "Got something here for . . ."

Tess perked up as Dee rifled through the bag of letters, parcels, and postcards she carried. She picked out two small packages.

". . . Ella and Peggy," she said, handing them to the excited girls. "Oh, and Tess, you have a postcard."

"Great," Tess mumbled, sounding far from happy. "My mom's assistant sent me a postcard."

"See ya around, girls!" Dee called as she left.

Ella tore into her care package to discover an assortment of goodies. Peggy pulled out her own treats.

"Uh, hello," Tess said, irritated, "back to the plan. We need to figure out how to have face time with Shane."

"Why don't we just take all his classes?" Ella suggested.

Tess brightened, like she'd just thought of

something. "Why don't we just take all his classes?" she repeated, claiming Ella's idea as her own. "I'm *so* 'smart girl' right now. Let's go and sign up."

Tess glanced quickly in the mirror, checking her makeup, then skipped out of the cabin. Ella and Peggy gave each other a look and dutifully followed.

Shane stared at the piece of paper he was holding. He shook his head. "I don't need a chaperone, Unc."

Brown sighed. "Seeing how you blew off your class yesterday, you sorta do."

"I didn't sign up for this. Get my agent on the phone," Shane demanded.

Brown gave his nephew a searching look. "What happened to you, man? That guy on TV? That's not who you really are." He pointed to Shane's heart. "*In there.* What happened to that kid who loved music?"

Shane avoided his uncle's eyes. "He grew up," he said, almost bitterly.

"Big whoop. Stop acting like it's all about you," Brown said, frustrated now.

"In my world, it is," Shane responded. He barely remembered a time when people didn't do everything he asked.

"We're in *my* world," countered Brown. "And in *my* world, you are considered an instructor at this camp. Which means you've got to instruct. Starting with Hip-Hop Dance at two."

With that, Brown gave his nephew a stern look and left him alone.

Inside the camp dance studio some of the campers were messing around, dancing freestyle and loosening up. But Tess, Ella, and Peggy hung back, waiting for class to start before busting out their moves.

"Now, remember," Tess whispered to her cohorts, "when he gets here, act cool." She leaned casually against the mirrors and tried to look chill.

Mitchie ran up, leaning over to catch her breath. "When who gets here?" she asked, having caught the end of Tess's comment.

"Shane," answered Ella.

Mitchie's face fell. "He's teaching this class? Great," she whispered under her breath. *What if he remembers me from the kitchen?*

Ella glanced over at Mitchie. She frowned. "Is that flour in your hair?" she asked.

Mitchie's eyes grew wide. She had to think fast! "No, uh, Chinese body powder. Cool, huh?" she managed.

At that moment, Shane entered the studio. Barely bothering to get everyone's name, he walked over to the stereo and pressed PLAY. Music filled the room. Counting off, Shane launched into a complex, choreographed number.

"He calls this teaching?" Mitchie muttered as she tried to take in the moves.

"It's a way to weed out the weak," Tess said matter-of-factly. She began to dance.

Mitchie sighed and started to move to the beat, too. Unlike some of the campers, she had little trouble keeping up—until Shane smiled at her. *Does he recognize me?* she worried, tripping over her feet and bumping into Tess.

"Hey!" Tess cried.

"Sorry," Mitchie muttered, trying to get back in step.

Next to her, Andy, his drumsticks poking out of his pocket, was doing far worse. He was all over the place.

"Eight! And one, two, three, four—" Shane continued to count out the beat, wincing at their out-of-sync performance. "Stop! Stop!" he finally yelled, punching the STOP button on the stereo.

"Talk about dancing to the beat of a different drum." Tess snickered, nodding at Andy. Some of the kids laughed, but Shane didn't notice.

"Hey," Shane said to Andy, gesturing to the sticks still in the boy's pocket. "You any good on the drums?"

Instead of answering, Andy pulled out his drumsticks and started tapping a rousing combination on a nearby bench. Shane nodded, impressed.

"Now we just have to work on getting that beat from those sticks to those feet," Shane joked.

Andy smiled. So did Mitchie. Maybe, she thought, there was more to Shane Gray than his obnoxious bad-boy, pop-star image suggested.

CHAPTER EIGHT

It was early—again—when Mitchie's alarm went off. She thought she managed to sneak out of the Vibe Cabin without waking up the other girls, but she didn't go altogether unnoticed. From her bed, Tess watched Mitchie and wondered just what was going on.

By midmorning, Mitchie was wiped out. Her double duty and early wake-up calls were beginning to wear on her. She ran from the kitchen, around the mess hall, and in again through the front door, plopping down next to

Tess, Ella, and Peggy, who were already eating breakfast.

"Where were you this morning?" Tess asked, as if she were accusing Mitchie of something.

Before she could answer, Mitchie saw her mother crossing the mess hall toward them. "Oh, no," she said under her breath.

"Hi, girls." Connie smiled at them.

"Uh . . . hi," said Tess.

"Hi. Uh, so . . . yummy breakfast," Mitchie said, sending her mother desperate mental messages not to blow her cover.

"How would you know?" her mom chided. "There's hardly anything on your plate."

Mitchie gave her a look that said, "Please be cool." Connie caught her drift and dropped it.

"Morning carbs," Tess said haughtily. "Definite no-no."

"Um, yeah," Mitchie agreed.

Connie bit her tongue and smiled. "I just wanted to meet Mitchie's new friends."

Mitchie introduced the girls. "This is Tess, Peggy, Ella."

"Hi," Peggy and Ella said in unison.

Tess was clearly not into it. "Yeah, hi. Again," she said, then turned away, not one to waste time on "the help."

Connie was taken aback by Tess's attitude. "Well, looks like you girls are busy. I'll talk to you later," she said before leaving.

"Okay," Tess said, raising an eyebrow, "what's up with random kitchen lady? Do you know her?" she asked Mitchie.

"Huh? I mean, don't you? She's cooked for everybody from Jessica and Nick pre-breakup to Pharrel."

"Really?" Ella asked, looking at her plate in a whole new light.

Mitchie nodded. "I'm shocked the camp got her," she continued. Nice save, she thought to herself.

"You mean Jessica ate these eggs?" Peggy wondered.

Mitchie nodded again, and Peggy and Ella chowed down.

Holding back a sigh of relief, Mitchie

picked up her fork. Her secret was still safe—for now.

"So, your friends seem nice," Connie said later that afternoon as she and Mitchie prepared dinner. "Tess is . . . interesting."

Mitchie rolled her eyes. "She's better once you get to know her."

Connie pursed her lips, then said, "She just doesn't seem like she's your type. You've always been—"

"Invisible," Mitchie inserted.

"I was going to say independent." Connie looked at her daughter, about to say more. But the moment was ruined by the oven buzzer. "Better hurry up and finish those potatoes if you want to get to the campfire!"

Mitchie peeled faster.

In his room in Brown's cabin, Shane strummed his guitar. He was playing a tune that had stuck in his head since the day outside the mess hall—Mitchie's song.

Brown appeared at the door. "That's cool." He smiled. "Like your old stuff."

Shane kept strumming. "Yeah. I was thinking maybe the group could change up our sound. Do something different."

His uncle nodded. This was progress. Not wanting to push it, he shifted gears. "So are you coming to the campfire?"

"Yeah, right." Shane scoffed at the idea.

"Okay. Sit in here by yourself, superstar," Brown said, disappointed yet again as he went to join the campers.

Shane sat on his bed and played his guitar alone. It wasn't that he didn't want to go; his ego was just blocking the way.

Across camp, the flames of a bonfire touched the starry night sky.

On the stage set up nearby, Dee addressed the crowd. "So tonight is what we call Campfire Jam. It's about expression. The freedom to be who you are."

The kids applauded and cheered.

"Who's up first?" she asked.

Tons of hands shot up, and soon the first act took the stage.

Tess, Peggy, and Ella stood near the back of the stage, waiting for their turn.

"Where is Mitchie?" Peggy asked.

"Right here," Mitchie said, running up and joining the group.

Brown approached them. "You girls are up next. Rock it!"

As Brown turned to go speak with Dee, he noticed his nephew walking up. Shane propped himself against a tree, away from the campfire, his hands stuffed into his pockets. It was a small step, but it was still a step. Brown smiled.

"Okay. Let's do it," Tess said.

The crowd watched as Tess, Mitchie, Ella, and Peggy took the stage. Tess stepped forward and tapped the microphone, which made a loud thumping noise. Catching sight of Shane, she covered the mike and whispered, "He's watching. Don't mess up." Then she cued

Barron and Sander at the soundboard and the music started.

Tess sang loud and big, as always, her eyes never leaving Shane. Behind her, Mitchie, Ella, and Peggy shimmied and shook and "oooh'd" and "ahhh'd."

When the song came to an end, the crowd broke into loud applause. At his spot by the tree, Shane's hands stayed in his pockets.

His thoughts were interrupted by two boys who didn't see him in the shadows. "Shane Gray is so played," the first one said as they passed.

"Not if you like that cookie-cutter pop-star garbage," said the other one. "I heard he's going to lose his contract."

"I hope so," the first one said. "Gift to my ears."

They laughed, unaware that Shane had heard everything. His face—and pride—burning, he turned and walked away.

Tess saw Shane leaving and cocked her head. Had he hated their performance? There was no time to wonder, though, as she walked off the stage and practically bumped into Caitlyn, who was waiting in the wings with her laptop.

Catching Mitchie's eye, Caitlyn gave her a long look. "Enjoy singing backup?" she asked sarcastically.

Mitchie didn't answer. Lowering her head, she walked away, Caitlyn's words ringing in her ears.

Mitchie was still upset by Caitlyn's remark as she made her way down one of the paths by the lake the next day. Suddenly, she heard singing— good singing. Following the voice, she came to the director's cabin. Shane was sitting on the steps, strumming a guitar. Hearing footsteps, he stopped.

"Can't a guy get some peace?" Shane groaned. Looking up, he saw that the intruder was Mitchie—one of the girls in his hip-hop class.

"Sorry," Mitchie said, ducking to turn away, then turning back. "Was that you singing? It was kinda . . . different."

"Than my usual cookie-cutter pop-star

stuff?" Shane asked sarcastically. The words the guys at the bonfire had said were echoing in his head. "Sorry to disappoint." He went back to picking his guitar.

"You didn't," Mitchie said quickly. "I liked it. It was good for stupid cookie-cutter star stuff."

She smiled and so did he. He set the guitar down. "Thanks," he said. "You really know how to make a guy feel better."

"I thought you loved your sound." Mitchie frowned. "You created it here. You're, like, a Camp Rock legend."

Shane heaved a heavy sigh. "Some legend. I play the music the label thinks will sell."

Mitchie leaned on the banister of the cabin porch. "You don't think that song would sell?"

Shane considered Mitchie's question. "I don't know," he said finally.

"Well," said Mitchie, swinging on the porch post, "you'll never know unless you try." She smiled. "And by the way, I know one girl who would buy that song." Turning, she disappeared down the path.

CHAPTER NINE

Another day, another lunch at Camp Rock. Mitchie, Tess, Ella, and Peggy carried their trays to their table. They passed Caitlyn working on her laptop, absentmindedly splaying her legs into the aisle.

Tess looked down, but it was too late. She tripped over Caitlyn's foot and teetered forward, her tray perilously close to spilling its contents. At the last second, she caught herself.

"Oops. Sorry," Caitlyn said. "Actually, I'm not."

"I would respond, but . . ." Tess's words trailed

off as if what she was about to say was just too horrible to be uttered aloud.

"But you are responding by saying you're not responding," Ella pointed out.

"Shut up," hissed Tess.

Tess started to move on, but as she did so, her tray tipped ever so slightly. Some of her food spilled off her plate and onto Caitlyn.

"Hey! That was on purpose!" Caitlyn cried out, wiping food from her pant leg.

"Does it matter?" asked Tess innocently. "Anything makes that outfit look better." She tilted her tray once again, and more food spilled. "See?"

Caitlyn had had enough. Grabbing a handful of noodles from her plate, she flung them at Tess.

"Hey, guys, stop!" Mitchie pleaded, trying to put an end to things before they got out of control. But it was too late for that—the noodles Caitlyn had thrown hit Mitchie.

"Oops. My spaghetti slipped," Caitlyn said.

"I can't believe you did that!" Tess yelled.

Caitlyn did it again. She laughed.

But her laughter stopped immediately when a familiar voice spoke up.

"Neither can I," said Brown.

Turning, Mitchie, Tess, and Caitlyn found themselves staring at one very *un*happy camp director. He raised a hand and pointed at the three of them. They were in big trouble.

Inside the director's cabin, Brown paced in front of Mitchie, Tess, and Caitlyn. The three girls stood before him, silently dripping food remnants on the cabin floor.

Finally, after what felt like an eternity, Brown stopped pacing and sighed. "Lay it on me," he said.

Caitlyn and Tess began screaming at the same time.

"She has always been jealous of me. She cannot stand the fact that I am probably going to win Final Jam, and she just started flinging food at me. I'm going to have my dad sue. These are Gucci shoes!" Tess screeched.

"She's impossible. She walks around here like

she owns the place, and why? Because her mom has some Grammys. So when she 'spilled' food on me, I lost it," Caitlyn yelled over her.

"Enough!" Brown bellowed. The girls fell into a strained silence. They'd never heard Brown raise his voice. "Who was the first one to throw food?" He tried again.

Tess smiled. "That's easy. Caitlyn."

Caitlyn turned and looked at Mitchie, silently asking her to stand up and tell the truth. Mitchie's eyes dropped to the ground.

"That's technically true," Caitlyn started, "but—"

"No 'buts,'" Brown cut her off. "Since you want to play with food," Brown went on, facing Caitlyn, "I can hook you up with a job in the kitchen. From here on out, you are on kitchen duty."

"What?" Mitchie blurted out. If Caitlyn came to work in the kitchen, she would totally find out Mitchie's secret! "I mean, ewww," she said when everyone looked at her.

"But—" Caitlyn began to object.

Brown put his hand up. "Again with the 'buts.' Look, it's settled." And with that, he exited the cabin, leaving two upset girls and one smug one in his wake.

The next day, Mitchie found herself, a box full of potato chips in hand, racing down one of the camp's paths. With her eyes focused on the ground, she didn't notice Shane until she practically bumped into him.

Shane looked at her, then at her chips, and then back at her. A smile spread across his face. "Hungry?" he teased.

"Just a little bit," Mitchie said, smiling back at him.

There was an awkward moment as Shane and Mitchie both stood smiling and nodding, unsure of what to say.

"You got a minute?" Shane asked, breaking the silence. "I wanna run something by you."

Mitchie gazed down the path toward the kitchen. I should be getting back to my mom, she thought. Then she looked back at Shane.

"Uh, sure," she said. She could spare a minute. After all, it was Shane Gray.

He gestured to a spot off the path and Mitchie followed, potato chips in tow.

A moment later, Mitchie was getting her own unplugged Shane Gray performance. She listened, impressed. The song was good. Unlike his usual stuff, this music was soulful and unique, raw with emotion. Shane played the last couple of chords and looked up at Mitchie.

"I heard this girl singing, and it kind of reminded me of the music that I like." In fact, Shane had been haunted by the girl's sound— little did he know, Mitchie's sound—since he'd heard it. "So I just started playing around with some chords. I know it's not finished, but—" he stopped, suddenly shy.

"No. It's really good," Mitchie assured him. Whoever the girl was, she had definitely made an impact. For a moment, Mitchie wished it had been her. But that was silly thinking . . .

Shane stared at Mitchie. He was so used to girls just screaming that he had forgotten what it was like to actually talk to one.

"Why are you looking at me like that?" Mitchie asked, blushing under his gaze.

"I don't know," Shane answered. "You seem different."

Mitchie laughed. Shane had no idea just how different she was. But did she dare tell him the truth? Maybe he would understand. She opened her mouth to speak, but then Shane smiled wider and Mitchie changed her mind.

Now wasn't the time. Maybe later . . .

Tess was walking on one of the paths that crossed by the spot where Mitchie and Shane were talking. She had her cell phone pressed to her ear.

"Camp is great, Cynthia. . . . Okay, when mom gets out of the studio, can you tell her I called again and that I love her?"

Not surprisingly, Tess hadn't heard from her mom in days. T.J. Tyler was in the midst of one of her "creative streaks," during which she didn't like to be bothered.

Looking up as she clicked the phone shut, her mouth dropped open. Mitchie and Shane were in the middle of the woods—together.

"So, I'd better get going," Tess heard Mitchie say.

"To the kitchen?" Shane asked.

"Huh?" Mitchie responded, taken off-guard. Did he know?

He pointed to the chips. "To get some dip for those."

"Oh, yeah, right."

They both laughed, like old friends would at an inside joke.

Mitchie felt her heart race. This was good. Very good.

Up on the path, Tess watched. This was bad. Very bad.

CHAPTER TEN

"**H**ey, Mom," Mitchie greeted her mother dreamily as she entered the kitchen. "How ya doing?"

Connie looked up from chopping a head of iceberg lettuce. "I'm all right," she said, amused by her daughter's mood. "How are you?"

"I'm great," Mitchie said, tying on her apron. "Fantastic. Wonderful. I'm—"

"—putting those chips in bowls," her mother instructed.

"Right." Mitchie headed to the pantry just as Caitlyn entered.

"Caitlyn," said Connie. "Thanks for coming in early. Taco night takes our six hands."

"Six?" Caitlyn asked, seeing only herself and Connie.

"My daughter," Connie explained. "So can you get started on the onions? Brown wants to talk to me about next week's campfire pig-out."

"Sure," said Caitlyn, putting on an apron and trying to get excited.

Thanking her, Connie left to find Brown, just as Mitchie reentered from the pantry with another big bag of chips. She spotted Caitlyn in just enough time to raise the bag to cover her face.

"Hey, you must be hands five and six," Caitlyn joked. "I didn't know Connie had a daughter. I'm Caitlyn."

Mitchie remained silent, afraid her voice would betray her. Instead, the bag of chips silently nodded hello. Mitchie's mind raced as she tried to plot an escape.

"Need some help?" Caitlyn asked.

The bag of chips shook no and backed toward the door. Turning, Mitchie bolted.

But she didn't get far. She ran smack into a bucket full of soapy water. With a shriek, Mitchie tripped and fell, spilling chips everywhere.

"Mitchie?" Caitlyn asked, running up.

Mitchie looked at Caitlyn but remained mute. She didn't know what to say or how to explain. It wouldn't sound right.

"Wait a minute," Caitlyn said, suddenly realizing what was going on. "You're the cook's daughter," she said incredulously. "She's your mom? Oh, this is rich . . . but apparently you're not."

"So, what are you waiting for?" Mitchie exclaimed, visibly upset. "Run. Go tell everybody."

Caitlyn folded her arms across her chest and looked down at Mitchie. "Maybe I should."

"Fine," Mitchie declared. "Whatever." She got up and started to uselessly wring out her

Mitchie has arrived at Camp Rock! The only
downside—she has to help her mother in the kitchen.

Tess, the diva of Camp Rock, is determined to win
Final Jam—and Shane Gray's heart.

When Mitchie sings her song in class, Brown lets
her know she's truly rockin'!

Shane Gray, the lead singer of Connect Three,
has some serious attitude.

Shane shows the class some of his
trademark pop-star moves.

Tess discovers Mitchie's secret! Mitchie's mom isn't
a superfamous record exec—she's the camp cook!

Shane is beginning to wonder if he'll ever
find "the voice."

Mitchie's busted! After Tess tells everyone Mitchie's secret,
the summer looks like it's going to get too hot to handle.

Tess blames Mitchie and Caitlyn for stealing her charm
bracelet. Now the two friends are banned from Final Jam!

With nothing better to do, Caitlyn blows up
balloons for that evening's jam.

Shane tells his uncle Brown about the mysterious girl
with the beautiful voice.

Shane and Mitchie finally get their own
moment to shine.

shirt, sending bits of chips flying.

Caitlyn gave her a hard look. "How long did you think you could keep your little secret?"

"Longer than this," Mitchie grumbled.

Bending down, Mitchie began picking chips up off the floor. The room was silent save for the occasional crunch of a chip as it broke in Mitchie's shaking hands.

"Why?" Caitlyn finally asked.

"Why do you care?" Mitchie responded curtly.

"I don't," Caitlyn said. "But when I tell everybody, I want the whole back story."

Mitchie narrowed her eyes. "I just wanted to fit in, okay?" Why can't the ground open up and swallow me completely? she thought.

"I think your whole charade is stupid and immature," Caitlyn announced. "Hiding behind some crazy lie."

"You hide, too," Mitchie said, suddenly defensive. "The 'I don't care about anything' attitude. If you don't care, why are you here?"

There was a moment of recognition between the two girls, a common ground they hadn't seen before. But the moment ended when Connie entered and got an eyeful of Mitchie's wet clothes.

"What happened to you?" she asked, startled.

"She drowned in her lies," Caitlyn muttered to herself.

"What?" Connie asked.

Mitchie looked at Caitlyn out of the corner of her eye, waiting for her to spell it all out for her mother—that her daughter was embarrassed about being the cook's daughter and had lied—to everyone.

Caitlyn returned Mitchie's look. "Nothing," she said, and then left the kitchen.

Tess ignored her lunch and flipped through the latest issue of a pop-star magazine. A picture of Shane caught her eye, and she stopped to quickly scan the article.

"Says here," Tess said, "*I'm* Shane's type. It's just a matter of time."

At that moment, Caitlyn walked by and glanced down at the glossy magazine. She saw

Shane's description of what he was looking for in a girl.

"'Warm, funny, talented,'" she read. She looked back at Tess. "You?"

Tess's blue eyes glared at Caitlyn, cold as ice, and she closed the magazine. Satisfied with the reaction, Caitlyn continued on and sat down at a nearby table, opening her laptop.

"Hey, guys. What are you doing?" Mitchie came up and sat next to Peggy and Ella. She took a bite of food.

"The question is what were *you* doing?" Tess asked, crossing her arms. "You're always AWOL."

"Huh?" Mitchie asked, feigning ignorance.

"Hey, Mitchie," Ella said, unwittingly coming to the rescue. "I was thinking, after camp, maybe we can come to visit you and your mom in China and go to that Happy Summer store."

"Uh, sure," she mumbled, then saw Caitlyn sitting alone, within earshot. Caitlyn was staring at her. Mitchie waited for her to say something, but she stayed silent. Mitchie was relieved . . . for the moment.

Tess, her annoyance apparently over, turned to the group. "Okay guys, tonight is the Pajama Jam. So, outfit check: green tees and white shorts." She noticed the girls' confused looks. "What? Green is Shane's favorite color. It was in the magazine!"

Pajama Jam was in full swing. Campers were dressed in an assortment of sleepwear: night-gowns, robes, pajama sets, boxer shorts, one guy was even wearing a fleece pajama suit complete with feet. In the middle of it all, a couple of counselors did the last steps in an intricate dance routine that ended to much applause.

As the sound of clapping died down, Mitchie appeared in the planned combo: green T-shirt and white shorts. As she searched for the girls in the crowd, she passed Caitlyn.

"The other lemmings are over there," Caitlyn noted sarcastically. She pointed to where Ella and Peggy stood in identical outfits.

Mitchie felt bad. She hated lying. It made her feel awful. But what could she do? If her secret got out . . . "Look, Caitlyn, about—"

Caitlyn cut her off. "Save it, Mitchie. . . . If that's even your real name."

Giving up, Mitchie went to join Peggy and Ella. The three were laughing at Brown's pajamas when Tess came up. She was not wearing the required green T-shirt and white shorts. Instead, she wore a short green night-gown.

"Are we ready?" she asked, smoothing her straps.

"Where's your T-shirt and shorts?" asked Mitchie, annoyed.

"Yeah, I thought we were going to wear the same thing," Peggy said.

"The backup singers should wear the same thing," explained Tess impatiently. "Not the lead singer. Hello?"

Peggy was about to say more when Dee took the mike. "Next up, Caitlyn." Her voice reverberated over the sound system.

Walking onto the stage, Caitlyn plugged her computer into the speakers and began to mix music and play the keyboard. Like most of the campers there, she was good. Really good, and Mitchie said so.

Tess said nothing and glowered at Caitlyn onstage.

"Hey, Shane likes her, too," Ella observed.

The girls turned to see that Shane had joined the crowd and was watching. He nodded his head to the music, oblivious to the stares from the girls around him.

Tess looked from Shane, to Caitlyn onstage, then back at Shane.

"Help!" she suddenly screamed at the top of her lungs. "Help! Snake!"

Everyone turned to Tess. Caitlyn, suddenly without an audience, stopped the music. Tess pointed to something coiled up at the edge of the lake nearby.

"Snake!" she screeched again.

Dee ran over, but when she saw Tess's "snake," she relaxed. "That's the swim line, Tess," she said, irritated.

"Oh, right." Tess put her hand to her heart

and tried to look innocent. "My bad."

Shaking her head, Dee left to check on the next performer.

Tess turned to Mitchie, Ella, and Peggy. "Sure looked like a snake." She shrugged smugly.

"You're so full of it." It was Caitlyn's voice. She had left the stage and was standing, her arms crossed, glaring at Tess.

"What's your problem?" Tess asked.

Caitlyn was steaming. "You." She practically spat out the word. "I know what you just did."

"What?" Tess said, taunting Caitlyn.

Caitlyn's nostrils flared as she tried to control her anger. "You can't stand that people might actually like what other people do."

"You mean your little duet with your laptop?" Tess sneered. "Uh, Boringville called. They want their leader back." She laughed, and Ella and Peggy joined in. Mitchie stayed silent.

"You make me so ill," said Caitlyn, who looked like she might really enjoy throwing up all over Tess's designer shoes.

Tess made an elaborate hand gesture. She put

up three fingers, and waving her wrist, formed a *W*, *E*, *M*, and *L*.

"Okay, what is that?" Caitlyn asked.

"She said, 'what*ever*, major loser'," Ella explained proudly.

The girls laughed again, and even though she tried to hide it, Caitlyn was clearly hurt. Mitchie could see it. And she could also see that Tess didn't care. Not one tiny bit. It made Mitchie feel ill, too.

"Wow, Tess," Mitchie blurted before she knew what she was saying. "'Whatever, major loser' is so last year. Everyone knows that . . . Well, I guess not everyone."

This time, Mitchie laughed. Ella and Peggy joined in, unable to help themselves. Tess, taken off balance by this turning of the tables, stormed away.

Looking over, Caitlyn gave the briefest of nods, just short of a "thank you."

CHAPTER ELEVEN

In the kitchen the next day, Mitchie and Caitlyn blew up balloons for that night's theme party in silence. Connie entered, holding a large cookie with a hole in the center. "Do these look like records?" she asked hopefully.

"Huh?" Mitchie grunted, confused.

"I mean CDs," Connie corrected herself for the twenty-first century. "Do these cookies look like CDs? I want to make sure they look authentic next to my 'quarter-note cupcakes.'"

"Everything looks great, Connie!" Caitlyn

reassured her as she tied off another balloon.

"These theme nights are the busiest," Connie said, shaking her head. "Oh! I'd better go get the ice cream." She rushed off, leaving the two girls alone again.

They both maintained their awkward silence, until Mitchie finally broke. "Did you sign up for Final Jam?" she asked.

Caitlyn nodded.

"So what are you going to do?"

Caitlyn looked suspiciously at Mitchie. "This is freaking me out. Why are we talking?"

"I don't know. Maybe I'm slumming," Mitchie said teasingly. She reached out and popped one of Caitlyn's balloons. Mitchie laughed. "Or maybe I wanted to set you up for *that*."

"Hey!" Caitlyn cried, but her scowl had softened into a smile. She grabbed a balloon and whacked Mitchie over the head. There was a brief, stunned pause before both girls burst into laughter and began whacking each other on the head and arms with the inflated balloons.

They finally settled into contented giggles. Then, Caitlyn surprised Mitchie by saying, "It's fun being friends with Tess."

"How would you know?" Mitchie asked.

"Because I was friends with Tess," Caitlyn explained. Catching Mitchie's skeptical look, she went on. "I know. Hard to believe."

"More like impossible. What happened?"

Caitlyn gave a heavy sigh. "Tess doesn't like competition and she felt I was," she explained. "With her, there can only be one star—herself. I know it's cool being her friend. I mean, she can make you feel so important. And she's popular, but so what?"

"Oh, come on." Mitchie rolled her eyes. "Being popular is so not a 'so what.'"

"No," Caitlyn admitted. "There are perks."

"Like . . . like . . ." Mitchie tried to think of one.

"Like singing backup for Tess all the time," Caitlyn offered. "Like never getting to say what you really feel. Oh, and those exciting shorts outfits?" She laughed. "Those were real high points. You're right. Sell your soul."

Mitchie halfheartedly hit Caitlyn with a balloon. But Caitlyn made some good points. Was being popular worth all of Tess's heckling?

"Hey," Caitlyn said, "I'm on your side."

Mitchie smiled and then noticed the time on the wall clock. She jumped up. "Shoot!" she exclaimed. "I was supposed to go meet—"

Caitlyn raised an eyebrow.

"We're practicing for the Final Jam," Mitchie said defensively.

Caitlyn made a mock flourish. "Of course. Her Highness awaits."

Mitchie grabbed her things and guiltily headed to meet Tess and the girls. Caitlyn's words were ringing in her ears.

Shane was also practicing. He'd been writing in his room all day. Since he'd heard that girl's song outside the mess hall, he couldn't shake it. Absentmindedly, he began to strum the song on his guitar.

His strumming was interrupted by the

loud shrill of his cell phone. The caller ID told him it was Nate. Putting the phone to his ear, he heard the sounds of splashing and shrieking. His bandmates were obviously enjoying themselves poolside.

"So, how's my birdhouse coming?" Jason asked over the speakerphone.

On the other end of the line, Shane rolled his eyes. He was *not* in the mood for this. "Guys—" he began.

"Sorry," Nate and Jason said in unison.

Another girl shrieked in the background and Shane winced. It was nothing like the soothing sounds of his mystery girl. Suddenly, Nate's words from the limo came back to him, and a smile spread across Shane's face.

"About me recording with a camper—" he began.

"You gotta do it, man," Nate said. "No go-backs."

"Actually, I've been thinking," Shane went on, much to his bandmate's surprise. "And I think it's cool."

"Man, are you feeling okay?" Nate asked. "Are you getting too much sun?"

"I'm fine," Shane said. "And remember, whoever wins, no go-backs."

Shane hung up before the guys could answer. "Now, I just have to find that girl from the mess hall," he said aloud to himself.

Glancing out the room's window, he saw Andy practicing a dance move. Hmm . . . maybe he could help.

Shane headed outside and made his way over to Andy. "Hey, buddy," Shane said. "You wanna do me a favor?"

Moments later, Andy was whispering Shane's message into a girl's ear. *"The girl with the voice,"* he said mysteriously.

Nodding excitedly, she immediately rushed to tell her friends. By afternoon, the rumor mill was working at full tilt. Shane smiled as he walked past a group of whispering campers. His plan was working. He would get to the bottom of the mystery voice—even if it meant using his pop-star pull. If "the voice" knew Shane was looking for her, she would have to come to him, right?

But then, out of nowhere a girl ran up, stopping abruptly in front of him and belting out the words to his first hit song.

She finished the chorus and looked at him hopefully. Shane smiled but shook his head. Nope, not her.

Another girl approached, this one with an operatic voice. Again, Shane shook his head.

Soon, a line had formed in front of Shane. It seemed every girl at Camp Rock was trying out. They all wanted to be "the girl with the voice."

Mitchie and Caitlyn, leaving the mess hall, stood and watched all the nervous girls practice their scales and warm up their voices.

"Aren't you going to get in line?" Caitlyn teased.

"It's not me." Mitchie shook her head emphatically. "He's never heard me sing." How could he have? she asked silently. I don't have the guts to get up in front—I'm always just backup.

To Shane's dismay, the tryouts continued. In the middle of that night, Shane was abruptly awakened by the sound of singing outside his window. The next day, working on his laptop in the mess hall, an instant message popped up with a streaming link of Ella singing.

But none of these voices were the one, and Shane was beginning to get discouraged.

CHAPTER TWELVE

It was a beautiful, sunny day, and Mitchie had decided to take the long way from the kitchen to the cabins. She was passing the lake when she thought she heard singing over the sound of birds and the lapping of water against the shore. She stopped and listened.

She recognized that voice—it was Shane's, and it was coming from a row of canoes tied to the dock. Mitchie tiptoed across the dock. Sure enough, Shane was slouched against one of the canoes, singing and jotting something on paper.

"So," Mitchie teased, "does your voice sound better over here?"

Shane grinned. "Why don't you get in and tell me," he gestured to the nearest canoe.

Mitchie climbed into the rocking boat, trying not to tip it over. Shane followed and then pushed off from the dock. They drifted out to the center of the lake, but then instead of moving forward, they started going in circles.

"I don't think we're doing this right," said Mitchie, dipping her oar into the cool, blue-green water.

"What? You don't like the circles?" he asked.

They both laughed. With the sun on her and the breeze lifting her hair, Mitchie felt herself relax. This was nice.

"So," Mitchie said, looking over with a sly smile. "Have you found your special girl?"

Shane returned the smile.

"Jealous?" he teased.

"Jerk," she retorted.

"Hey," Shane protested, "being a jerk is all part of the rock star image!"

"Keeping up an image can be tiring," Mitchie observed, thinking back to what she'd gone through so far this summer.

Shane looked down into the still water. "But it keeps the posers away," he observed. "I never know if people are hanging out with me for the parties or the free stuff."

"Definitely the free stuff," Mitchie said, joking.

Shane smiled. "It's probably the same with you, huh?" he asked.

Mitchie looked confused.

"Because of your mother and her big job. People must be fake around you, too."

Mitchie dipped her hand in the water, letting the drops roll off her fingertips. She should tell him the truth. It was now, or never. . . .

"Right," she said instead, letting the moment pass. "Um, totally."

"It's nice talking to someone who gets it," Shane said, sounding almost shy.

"Yeah," Mitchie replied.

Who am I kidding? Mitchie thought. Shane

would never forgive me if he found out I was just like all the other liars and fakes.

She picked up her oar and began to paddle again, oblivious to the fact that Tess had also taken the long way home. She watched Mitchie and Shane from the shore, and she was *not* happy.

Tess was still fuming when she found herself walking by the kitchen entrance later. She came to a stop when she heard familiar laughing from inside. The screen door creaked open, and Tess hid behind a tree, watching as a giggling Mitchie and Caitlyn left the kitchen.

"Okay, Mom. We're done," Mitchie said over her shoulder.

From inside, Tess heard the now-familiar voice of Connie Torres—camp cook—answer. "You girls have fun at the campfire. Thanks again."

As Mitchie and Caitlyn ran up the path toward the campfire and the theme jam, Tess could barely contain a shout of delight. Oh, she thought, this was too good to be true. Mitchie wasn't a star, she was the help!

The campground was full of the sounds of excited chatter mixed with the occasional song or drumbeat. Mitchie and Caitlyn had made their way from the kitchen and found a spot with Ella, Peggy, Barron, and Sander.

"Hey, I've heard talk of s'mores," Barron said, rubbing his stomach.

"Oh, they're coming," Mitchie assured him with a laugh. But catching Caitlyn's warning look, she added, "Um . . . probably."

She was saved from further s'mores talk by the appearance of Tess. The smug look on her face was even more smug than usual as she smiled at Mitchie and asked her what was up.

"Nothing," Mitchie replied, a bit confused.

"Are you sure?" Tess asked.

Before Mitchie could respond, though, Brown and Shane walked onto the campground's stage. The campers broke into loud applause. Brown grabbed the mike as Shane stood off to the side.

"Hey, gang! I finally talked my nephew," Brown smiled at Shane, "into singing us a song."

The crowd went nuts. Mitchie smiled at Shane onstage; he smiled back. Tess caught their exchange, and her blood boiled.

Shane took the mike from Brown. "Okay, you guys, I've got a surprise." He paused for effect. "Guys, come on out."

From the wings, Nate and Jason walked onto the stage, instruments in hand. Although it hadn't seemed possible, the crowd went even wilder. The noise was earsplitting. Smiling, Shane hushed the crowd before going on. "We are trying something new. So, let us know what you think."

He nodded to Nate and Jason, strummed a note on his guitar, and began to sing. The song was beautiful and different, exactly the sound Mitchie had been encouraging him to experiment with. It was one hundred percent Shane, and it was one hundred percent awesome. Connect Three had never sounded better.

The crowd was loving it as they swayed to the music. Shane could sense their reaction and relaxed, getting even more into it. Although he seemed to be singing to the crowd, Shane was really singing to someone in particular—to Mitchie. And this was not lost on Tess.

When the song came to an end, there was a moment of silence before the audience erupted into thunderous applause. Shane smiled broadly and looked at Mitchie, whose smile was even bigger.

"Man, they loved it," Nate observed from up on the stage. "You were right."

Jason, mistakenly thinking Nate was talking to him, responded, "I know I was right." Then his brow furrowed. "What did I do?"

"Not you," Nate said. "Shane." Looking over at his bandmate, he added, "The label has to let us do this."

But Shane wasn't sure, and he said so.

Nate wasn't ready to give up, though. "We

can hit the studio tonight and get them a demo by tomorrow. They can't say no once they hear it."

Shane nodded, but his attention was not on the demo. He was looking across at Mitchie. "I can't just leave," he said finally. "I'm not finished here."

Following his gaze, Nate saw Mitchie, and a smile spread across his face. He understood. Shane had to do what he had to do. Promising they would see him at Final Jam, Nate and Jason left, and Shane made his way to Mitchie.

Tess, meanwhile, saw Shane going over and then saw Connie nearby. This was her chance. It was act now, or never be the star. Taking a deep breath, she turned to Mitchie and in a loud voice, asked, "Mitchie, tell us about your mom again."

Hearing Tess, some campers turned. Connie, also within earshot, paused and listened. Mitchie felt like a deer caught in the head-lights.

"Her mom is a great person," Caitlyn said,

jumping to Mitchie's rescue. "What's your mom like?" she asked, turning to Barron.

Barron was confused. "Um, she's like, a mom."

But Tess wasn't going to be swayed. She had zeroed in on Mitchie and wouldn't let her go until she was finished. "I mean, I know she's president of Hot Tunes TV China," she went on, louder this time. "But tell me again about how important she is."

Now everyone was listening. Connie looked at Tess and then at Mitchie. Mitchie dropped her head, ashamed. All eyes were on her. Brown and Dee, by the stage, exchanged confused looks.

Mitchie began to speak in a low, almost inaudible voice, "She . . . uh . . . she . . ." she squeaked.

"I'm sorry, what?" Tess egged her on.

"She . . . uh . . . she's pretty cool," Mitchie said, a little louder.

Tess was relishing this. "And?" she prompted.

"And . . . uh . . ." Mitchie stammered. She

looked for her mother, to try to make her understand that she hadn't meant to hurt her, but Connie had vanished. "She's not president of Hot Tunes TV China." Mitchie finally exhaled.

Tess faked shock. "What's that? She's not president? You mean you . . . lied? To everybody?"

"No," Mitchie said, trying to think how to explain this.

A ripple went through the crowd.

"So, she's what?" Tess continued. "Vice President? Treasurer?"

The kids waited breathlessly for Mitchie's answer.

"Tess," Caitlyn said sternly, having heard enough.

Tess shot Caitlyn a look. "Go on. Tell us." She bullied Mitchie.

Mitchie was almost in tears. "She's a cook," she said, wanting to swallow the words.

"A cook? At Hot Tunes China?" Tess said, in mock confusion.

"No. Here," Mitchie said, her shoulders slumped in humiliation and defeat.

This was all Tess wanted to hear. Her face broke into a satisfied grin.

"So, you lied," Tess said again to Mitchie. "Your mom cooks our food. And you help her. That's the only way you can afford this camp, right?"

Mitchie stood dumbfounded. She was embarrassed and ashamed at the truth, but mostly at herself for lying.

"You're a real jerk," Caitlyn hissed.

"Maybe," answered Tess. "But I'm not a big, fat liar." She pinned Mitchie with her eyes, then turned to Peggy and Ella. "Come on," she commanded.

Peggy and Ella gave Mitchie one last disappointed look before turning and following Tess. The other campers whispered among themselves. Mitchie could hear the words, "liar," "that's really sad," and "poser," drifting through the crowd. Some campers giggled and laughed.

"Mitchie . . ." Caitlyn started, moving to comfort her.

"It's okay." Mitchie shrugged her off. Shane, who'd heard everything, had just stepped in front of her. "Shane . . ." she started, tears welling up in her eyes.

"You were lying?" he asked, his voice hard.

"Yes, but I—"

"Wow," he said coldly. "You know, I'm used to people pretending around me—"

"I wasn't pretending," Mitchie interrupted, wishing she could explain. The last person she'd wanted to hurt was Shane.

"I really thought you were different. But you're just like everyone else. You wanted to be friends with 'Shane Gray,' not me. Trick's on me, huh?" He gave a forced laugh.

"I was just trying to—"

"Save it for your interview with *Star Scoop* magazine," he said. "I know I gave you an earful."

Shane kicked at the grass and walked away,

his guitar slung heavily over his shoulder. As Mitchie watched him go, the tears finally began to fall, salty and heavy.

"Not here, you don't," said Caitlyn. She grabbed Mitchie by the hand and whisked her away.

The next day, Shane sat on the porch of the director's cabin, gloomily strumming his guitar. He should have known better. Mitchie had seemed too good to be true because she was.

Looking up, he saw Brown ambling toward the cabin. What he didn't see was Tess, who had come to comfort him in his time of need. Catching sight of Brown, she dropped behind and listened, hidden in the shadows.

"So what happened last night?" Brown asked when he got to the porch.

"Nothing," Shane said shortly.

"It didn't look like nothing, mate. You looked crushed, pummeled, absolutely destroyed."

"I get it, Uncle Brown," Shane responded.

He had been there and didn't need a refresher. "I'm just going to focus on my music. Change my sound. I don't need to get sidetracked with liking someone too much, anyway."

Brown frowned. "Are you still looking for that girl?" he asked.

Shane gave him a surprised look.

Brown shrugged. "I'm plugged in to camp gossip."

"It's crazy," said Shane, still picking at the strings on his guitar. "Her song is stuck in my head." He sang a few lines and then faded into silence.

Tess, still hidden in the shadows, furrowed her brow. She'd heard those lyrics before. But where?

Moments later, Tess was back in her cabin and lifting Mitchie's mattress from the bed frame. Bingo! Underneath lay Mitchie's songbook. Tess pulled it out and flipped through the pages. Then she found it—the song Shane had been singing on the porch.

Tess read through the lyrics once, twice. Suddenly, it all made sense. Mitchie was the girl with the voice! But if Shane found out . . .

Tess thought for a second. Then she looked at her charm bracelet and back at the book. A sly smile spread across her face. She had a brilliant idea.

CHAPTER THIRTEEN

While Tess was scheming, Mitchie and Connie were walking . . . in silence. Finally Connie spoke. "I didn't know you felt so ashamed of yourself," she said sadly.

"I'm not ashamed," Mitchie said, and she meant it. "It's just that for once I wanted to fit in, be popular."

"What do you mean?" Connie said, turning to look at her daughter with concern. "You have plenty of friends at home."

Mitchie gave her a look. "I have one. And last I checked nobody was busting their butts to sit at the lunch table with us. When I got here, I wanted to have a different experience, just once."

She thought she'd cried herself dry, but Mitchie started to tear up again.

"Oh, sweetie," Connie said, pushing the hair from her daughter's forehead, "you are so much more than you see. You don't need to lie about who or what you are."

Mitchie gave her a forlorn look. She'd heard this talk before. Heck, she'd written songs about it herself!

"And I'm not just saying that because I'm your mother," Connie protested.

"Mom?"

"Okay, I admit I am biased. But it's true! You are talented. Your music speaks to people. People want to listen to you . . . and it's not just me and your dad!"

Mitchie smiled. If only she could believe that.

111

★ ★ ★

Campers milled around, waiting for Shane's dance class to start. He was late . . . again. They were laughing and still talking about the previous night. Then Mitchie entered, and the studio went silent except for a few muffled laughs.

Tess turned to Ella but spoke loud enough for Mitchie to hear. "What a joke," she said, rolling her eyes and turning her back on her old cabinmate and "friend."

As other campers laughed, Mitchie tried to act like she wasn't bothered, but inside she wanted to die.

Finally, Shane entered, and the class settled down. "So," he said, looking at Mitchie before quickly turning away, "Final Jam is coming up and I know you're all excited."

A chorus of "yeps" and "you know its" went up in response.

"Here is some advice," continued Shane. "It's not all about your image. None of it means anything unless people see who you really are." Now he looked directly at Mitchie. "Your music has to be who you really are. It's got to say what you feel. Or it doesn't mean anything."

Mitchie lowered her eyes and held back the tears.

Shane had made his point.

Later that afternoon, Mitchie picked her way through the crowded mess hall and finally took a seat at the table with Caitlyn, Lola, Barron, and Sander.

"You know, sitting with the kitchen help is really hurting my rep," Barron stated.

Mitchie started to apologize but then Lola spoke up. "What rep?" she asked, joking, and Mitchie breathed a sigh of relief. At least *some* people were talking to her.

But then Tess laughed at something from across the room, and Mitchie's shoulders tensed. "Believe me," Caitlyn said, "it's probably not that funny."

Abruptly, Tess got up and crossed the room, trailed by Peggy and Ella. She stopped when she reached Mitchie.

"The chicken was kind of dry," Tess said in a loud voice. Then, to Mitchie, "Who should I report that to?"

"Maybe it wasn't the chicken," said Lola with an attitude. "Maybe your mouth is dry from all the hot air coming out of it."

A few campers raised their eyebrows, but Tess didn't respond. Instead, she said to Mitchie, "Can you tell your mom to be a little more careful?"

Her insult successfully delivered, Tess turned to strut away.

As she watched Tess go, Mitchie found the strength she'd been looking for. She stood up.

"Tess?" Mitchie said in an unwavering voice. Tess turned and shot Mitchie a look that dared her to say something. "Stop talking to me like that," Mitchie continued defiantly. "Stop talking to *everyone* like that. I may be the cook's daughter, my father may not be rich, but I am a much better person than someone who feels better about herself because she makes everyone else feel bad. And I'll take that any day."

The room had grown silent. Everyone was

staring at Tess, whose cheeks were becoming bright pink. But always the consummate actress, she quickly regained her composure.

"Make something good for dinner," she hissed. "I'll be starving after practice. And by the way, if it wasn't obvious, you're *so* out of the group." Tess tossed her head and turned on her heel to go. Peggy and Ella followed dutifully.

Behind her, Caitlyn gave Mitchie a warm smile.

"Then we'll make our own group," said Caitlyn.

Mitchie nodded. She may have lost her social status, but being herself again was worth it.

A crowd was gathering behind him as Brown stapled a poster to the bulletin board outside the Mess Hall of Fame. In bright letters, it announced something the entire camp had been buzzing about since the first day: FINAL JAM: 5 DAYS.

For the next few days, camp was filled with the sounds of preparation. Groups sang, danced, drummed, and jumped as they got their groove on for the big jam. Tess, Ella, and Peggy were sweating as they drilled through their choreography. They weren't getting very far, however, as Tess stopped them every eight counts to chew the other girls out for one mistake or another.

Two days later, Brown had tacked up a 3 to cover the 5 on the poster. Three days till Final Jam, and on the campgrounds, Sander and Barron were practicing their rapping. In the Vibe Cabin, Tess was still lecturing an annoyed Peggy and Ella on their routine.

Two more days down, and Brown had replaced the 3 with a 1. It was the day before Final Jam, and Mitchie and Caitlyn quickly put away groceries so they could go practice their routine. When they were done in the kitchen, they went to the lake. They wanted all the practice they could get.

Later that day, Mitchie and Caitlyn were ready. Back in the kitchen, they were telling Connie a story as they stirred big vats of macaroni and cheese. Just then, the door flew open. It was Tess, followed by Brown.

"I'm sure they have it," Tess said, pointing an accusing finger first at Mitchie and then at Caitlyn.

The girls looked at one another, clueless as to what Tess was talking about. "Okay, she has officially lost it," Caitlyn said.

"No, I didn't lose anything," Tess insisted. "You stole it."

"What?" Mitchie asked.

Connie was just as confused. "What is going on here?" she asked.

Brown, who had been standing silently while Tess threw accusations, finally stepped forward. Taking a deep breath, he ran a hand over his light brown hair before speaking. "Tess thinks that Mitchie and Caitlyn took her charm bracelet."

"What?!" the two girls exclaimed at once.

Mitchie's mom shook her head confidently. "I'm sorry, Brown, but the girls would never do such a thing."

"Look," Brown said calmly, "let's just settle this." He thought if Tess looked for her "stolen" charm bracelet and could not find it, this would end quickly.

"But—" Mitchie protested. She hadn't taken anything!

Tess was still glaring and pointing at her. "I know it was her. She was lying all summer about who she is. Who knows what else she'd lie about?"

"Okay," said Brown, noting Caitlyn's angry stare and Mitchie's red cheeks. "We'll look here first and then in your cabin."

"Fine," Mitchie shrugged.

"Whatever," Caitlyn said between clenched teeth.

Glancing around the cluttered kitchen, Brown finally stepped up to the counter. He began opening drawers filled with utensils and cookware.

"See, you're not going to find anything, because we didn't—" Mitchie started to protest again, but stopped as Brown pulled something shiny from under a stack of cookbooks.

"That's my bracelet!" cried a triumphant Tess.

"There must be some mistake," said Connie.

"Like what? I snuck into the kitchen and left an expensive bracelet under a *coq au vin* recipe?" Tess said sarcastically.

"Tess, I got this," Brown said sternly. Turning to Mitchie and Caitlyn, he added, "I am totally wigging out." His wrinkled brow confirmed his dismay.

"So are we," said Mitchie.

"I'm not," Caitlyn snapped. She should have known that Tess would stop at nothing to get what she wanted, which was Mitchie out of her hair.

Brown sighed. "Since it's the end of camp, I have no choice. I've got to ban you guys from the rest of camp activities . . . until the end of Final Jam."

"She's lying!" Mitchie cried. "We didn't do anything!"

"I'm sorry. My hands are tied," Brown said, sounding sincere. *"Until the end of Final Jam,"* he repeated. Then, with one last parting look, he left.

Following behind him, Tess shot the girls an infuriating smirk that said it all. She had done exactly what she had come to do. Mission accomplished.

CHAPTER
FOURTEEN

Finally, the night of Final Jam arrived. All over camp, the sounds of singing, rapping, drumming, and various instruments could be heard—guitars, trumpets, keyboards, fiddles. Everywhere, that is, but in the kitchen, where Mitchie and Caitlyn were busy with another task—filling up ketchup containers. As if missing out on Final Jam wasn't punishment enough!

Outside, parents were arriving, greeted by

hugs and shouts of "You made it!" and "What took you so long?" Tess stood on the outskirts of the arrival chaos, scanning hopefully for her mother.

"Tess," Dee said, coming up behind her.

"Mom?" Tess turned, a big smile on her face. It disappeared when she saw Dee.

"Thirty minutes to curtain," Dee reminded softly. "Chop-chop."

"Right," Tess said. She dropped her disappointed face and put on a huge, forced smile. After all, she had a show to put on.

In his bedroom, Shane was also preparing for Final Jam. He was sliding his jacket over his shoulders when he heard a knock at the door. A moment later, it swung open and Nate and Jason entered the room.

"Hey, dude," Nate said.

"Guess who?" added Jason.

Shane paused to give his bandmate a look before answering. "Dude, you're in the room. I can see you."

Jason smiled. Then he pulled the two other guys into a big hug. He had missed the band being together. But after tonight they could go back to rocking again.

"So, good news," Nate said when the hugging was over. "The press is here and they're going to cover the whole night." He made an imaginary headline with his hands. "The label loves it."

Shane nodded. He wasn't surprised. The label would do anything to get some publicity.

"Where's this amazing singer you've been looking for?" Jason asked.

Shane gave him a look. How did Jason know about the girl with the voice?

"What?" asked Jason, shrugging. "I know things."

Shane smiled. His buddy always had a way of surprising him. "I'm hoping to find her tonight," he said, before turning and leaving the cabin.

Unfortunately, "the voice" was nowhere near the Final Jam. Mitchie sat by the lake with

Caitlyn, throwing rocks that landed with a loud *kerplunk*. Caitlyn angrily punched a key on her laptop, and music poured from the speakers.

"This was supposed to be a fun summer of playing music," Mitchie said, throwing another rock. The disappointment was obvious in Mitchie's voice. "And all I did was get caught up in Tess's drama."

"It happens." Caitlyn sighed. "I never saw Brown so harsh."

Mitchie nodded. He had been *so* adamant. "He just kept repeating *'until the end of Final Jam . . .'*" Mitchie said, mimicking the camp director.

"Uh, I know," replied Caitlyn, "I was there." Looking up from her laptop, she saw a gleam in Mitchie's eye. A gleam that sure didn't look like defeat.

Mitchie was up to something. But what?

Brown stood on the stage of the Final Jam theater, looking out at the crowd of parents and campers. Dee and some of the counselors passed out glow sticks, adding to the fun, party atmosphere. It was going to be a great night.

Clearing his throat, Brown began, "Okay, campers, friends, family, Camp Rock fans—this is it. Tonight, music history will be made as Camp Rock finds a new Final Jam winner!"

Cheers went up from the crowd. Some swiveled their glow sticks like spotlights, while others whistled loudly through their fingers.

"Now, this year, the Final Jam winner will not only get a Camp Rock trophy," Brown paused for effect, "he or she will get a sweet prize: a chance to record with my nephew, pop star Shane Gray!"

Once again, the crowd cheered but now the sounds of girls shrieking were mixed in. This was definitely big news. And then Brown dropped another bombshell. He introduced the judges for the evening—Connect Three! The noise rose to a deafening roar.

Brown waited for everyone to settle before finishing up his intro. "Now, remember," he said. "Hold up your glow sticks when you hear a song you like." Everyone waved their bright wands in the air. "All right, let's kick it into over-drive and get this jam rocking!"

While Brown got the crowd energized, Tess, Peggy, and Ella were at one side of the stage, still rehearsing. In fact, they were pretty hard to miss in their elaborate costumes. They were practicing a complicated dance move when Tess stopped them with a flick of her wrist.

"This is not amateur night," she said sharply. "This is serious."

Ella was exasperated. "We did it right!" she protested.

"No, you didn't," Tess shot back. "You never do. I'm trying to win. You may be used to losing, but not me. I'm really tired of taking up the slack."

Peggy's eyes nearly bulged out of her head. She'd had just about enough of Tess Tyler and her drama.

"Stop telling us what to do!" Peggy cried.

"*You're* the one who's ruining everything."

Turning her back on Tess, Peggy turned and walked off.

"Peggy. Come back here!" Tess yelled, her hands on her hips. But Peggy kept walking. Tess turned to Ella. "Who needs her? She was just holding us back."

Ella gulped. But then, she straightened up. "You know what?" she said. "Do it yourself. I'm done." Tess's face dropped. Turning to go, Ella added, "BTW, your lip gloss is so not glossy anymore." And with that, she followed Peggy and left a very angry Tess in the dust.

Outside Caitlyn's cabin, drama of a different sort was playing out. Mitchie nearly collided with Caitlyn as she ran up carrying a garment bag.

"You got everything?" Mitchie asked.

"Yep," nodded Caitlyn.

Mitchie's stomach twisted in nervous knots. "Cool," she smiled. Her plan was officially in motion.

★ ★ ★

Once again, Brown took the stage, this time to introduce the first act—the It Girls.

Taking a deep breath, Tess—minus the other It Girls—walked onto the stage. Scanning the crowd, her eyes stopped on Connect Three's table. She was about to shoot them a smile when she saw someone else—a glamorous woman, dressed like a movie star, taking her seat in the back row. People started to stir and crane their necks to see her as she stopped to sign autographs.

Tess's eyes lit up. "Mom?" she whispered, hardly believing her mother had really made it.

Reenergized, Tess snapped to and took her opening pose. The music started, and she began her routine, singing and dancing her heart out. Her eyes were glued to her mother in the audience, as if she was performing just for her. Tess jutted her hip, threw up her arm, and then spun and turned, focusing again on her mother . . . who was checking her cell phone. T.J. scooted out of the row to take a call. She wasn't even watching Tess anymore.

Tess deflated. She tried to keep up with the steps she'd practiced a hundred times, but her mind was elsewhere, and she missed a beat. She slipped and fell to the floor.

Trying to take it in stride, Tess sprang back to her feet, but she couldn't keep up. The magic was gone . . . and so was her mother. Letting out a strangled cry, Tess ran offstage.

Brown took the stage once again. After all, the show had to go on. He quickly introduced the next act—Barron James, Sander Loya, and the Hasta La Vista Crew.

The curtain opened to reveal the group, who quickly jumped into a hot reggaeton number. The crowd responded by surging to their feet. A few people held up their glow sticks, waving them into the darkening sky.

When their song was finished, several more acts followed until Brown once again took the stage. "Well," he said, "it looks like that's all for tonight—"

Suddenly, Dee ran up to him, handing him a scrap of paper. Brown read it, surprise coming over his face. "Seems like we have a last-minute addition," he announced. "Come on up, Margaret Dupree."

The crowd looked at each other and shrugged, clapping. Backstage, Ella was just as confused. "Who's Margaret?" she asked quietly.

"Me," Peggy answered, walking up to join her friend.

Ella nodded, smiling. "Go, Margaret!" she cheered as Peggy ran onto the stage and took her place in the spotlight.

When Peggy opened her mouth, a soulful, deep voice came out. Years of frustration at playing second fiddle to Tess poured out of her. She was amazing! She strutted up and down the stage, belting out her song with a confidence the crowd—including Connect Three—had never seen before.

In the audience, glow sticks were going crazy. The crowd loved Peggy and her energy. Finishing the song, she took a triumphant bow. As she ran off the stage, blowing kisses at the audience, Tess called out her name.

"What?" Peggy said, ready for a fight.

But Tess had no fight left in her. "You were really good," she said quietly. "And if you're good, somebody should tell you."

Peggy smiled. "Thanks."

Turning to go, Tess threw out one more surprise. "And I'm sorry," she said.

"I know, I know," Brown was saying from the stage, as he tried to settle the crowd still going wild from Peggy's showstopping performance. "I guess that's it. It's officially *the end of Final Jam*. And time for our judges to go off in private and, well, judge," he said gesturing to Connect Three. Shane, Nate, and Jason stood up and made their way to the back of the theater.

Brown turned to leave the stage, when all of a sudden, music blared from the speakers. The crowd, which had started to get up, quickly shuffled back to their seats. Looking over at the wings, Brown saw Mitchie and Caitlyn gesturing wildly to him. Trying to hide his smile, he walked over.

"It's the *end of Final Jam*," Mitchie said when he joined them.

"I hoped you would catch on," he said, letting his smile finally show. "Now, go out there and steal their hearts."

CHAPTER FIFTEEN

All the adrenaline that had been pumping through Mitchie's veins seemed to vanish as she walked to the center of the stage and saw all the people. The campers, their parents, Shane, and even the press were looking—and waiting. Out of the corner of her eye, she saw Caitlyn start the music. But when Mitchie opened her mouth to sing, she couldn't do it.

Caitlyn immediately restarted the song. Mitchie took a deep breath and finally started to sing—very quietly.

"Louder," Caitlyn whispered.

But Mitchie was so nervous, it was all she could do to remember the lyrics. She looked into the crowd, finding her mother and father. She started to sing louder. Then she spotted Shane, and her voice picked up until it was full-throated and strong.

Closing her eyes, Mitchie sang her song loud and clear. She sang what she had trouble saying—that she was so much more than meets the eye, and that she had found her dream and there was no way she would let it go ever again.

From his spot in the back of the theater, Shane's eyes grew wide. He couldn't believe it. "Hey, that's the song," he said.

"So that must be the girl," observed Nate.

Shane stared at Mitchie up on the stage, so confident and talented, so true. This was Mitchie's moment. Mesmerized, along with the rest of the audience, Shane began to make his way toward the stage. When he got close enough, he smiled at Mitchie. She returned the smile while continuing to sing.

Grabbing a mike from Brown, Shane ran up the stage stairs and joined Mitchie in the lyrics he now knew by heart. He looked into her brown eyes as they sang to each other. In that moment, all the lies and all the pretending were forgiven.

When they finished, they dropped their mikes but not their gazes. For a silent moment, Mitchie and Shane looked at each other as if for the first time. Then they were engulfed by roaring applause so loud it shook the stage. And while every glow stick in the audience was up and swinging, Mitchie and Shane continued to look into each other's eyes—oblivious to anyone but each other.

The crowd was antsy as they eagerly anticipated the announcement of the Final Jam winner.

Shane stood onstage with Brown and Dee but couldn't take his eyes off Mitchie, who waited eagerly in the wings with Caitlyn.

A young camper handed a sealed envelope

to Brown and then rushed offstage. "Okay, everyone," Brown announced, "this is it. The winner of Final Jam this year is . . ."

Brown ripped open the envelope. He was as eager as the campers to hear who had won. As he read, a grin crossed his face. "Margaret Dupree!" he said proudly.

Peggy clutched at her chest as if to say, "Who, me?" Her face went from a look of shock to joy. The crowd applauded wildly.

"You won! You won!" Mitchie screamed, jumping up and down.

"You gotta go! You gotta go!" Ella said, pushing her friend onto the stage.

Peggy didn't need to be told twice. She ran to the stage, and Brown handed her a huge Camp Rock trophy and an envelope.

"Way to go!" Brown grinned. "You just got yourself a chance to record with Shane Gray."

The crowd cheered.

"Congratulations, Peggy," said a smiling Shane. "You deserve it. You were amazing. I can't wait to record with you."

Shane and Peggy hugged and posed for the flashbulbs going off all around them.

Back in the wings, Mitchie couldn't stop smiling. "We did it," she said, throwing an arm around Caitlyn.

"*You* did it," Caitlyn corrected.

Mitchie's eyes widened as she let out an "I can't believe it!" scream. She *had* done it. She'd stood on her own two feet and sang her heart out to a huge audience. And they'd liked it! Mitchie couldn't wait to do it again.

In that moment, Tess appeared beside them. The air was tense as the girls waited for her to speak.

"You guys were great," Tess said finally. She even sounded sincere.

"Thanks," said Mitchie.

"Yeah," seconded Caitlyn, knowing how hard those words were for Tess.

Tess seemed uncomfortable. "So, I . . . uh . . . told Brown you guys didn't take my bracelet," she said, looking down at her feet.

"Thanks," Mitchie said again. There was

nothing left to say so Mitchie and Caitlyn left to find their family and friends. Tess stood alone.

"Hey, honey!" Tess heard behind her. She turned to see her mother walking toward her. "You were so good up there," T.J. said, putting her arm around Tess.

Tess shrugged her mother's arm off. "You didn't see it."

T.J. looked confused, then her face softened. "I did," she said proudly. "Got the whole thing on my camera phone."

"Really?" Tess's face brightened.

T.J. hugged her daughter tight. "How about you tell me all about camp on my tour bus while we're in Europe?"

Tess pulled away, her eyes shining, "I'm going on your tour?"

Her mom nodded. "I don't want to capture all our good times on my phone."

Tess smiled wide.

Mitchie had finally found her father and mother. "Sorry you didn't win," Connie said, giving her daughter a big hug.

"It wasn't about winning, Mom," Mitchie said with a grin.

As if on cue, Shane walked up. Mitchie gave her parents a knowing look and moved to the side, eager to hear what Shane had to say.

"I guess my search is over," he whispered, a smile lighting up his face.

"Depends on what you're looking for," Mitchie teased. Then, because she had never officially done it, Mitchie introduced herself.

"So," Shane went on after he introduced himself. "Up for a canoe ride later?"

"I wouldn't miss it," answered Mitchie.

Then they shared a smile bright enough to light up the night.

"**O**kay, everybody!" Brown called one more time from the Camp Rock stage. "Final Jam is over. And you know what that means—the Final Jam jam session!"

"Let's kick it!" yelled Dee.

A mix of music filled the air. It was rock and

roll, pop, R&B, reggae, country, opera, folk, heavy metal—all rolled into one, just like Camp Rock.

The campers swarmed the stage, even Mitchie and Shane. It was a full-on party, and they stood in the midst of it all, dancing and singing together. As the music swelled around them, Shane bent down and kissed Mitchie on the cheek. Blushing, Mitchie knew one thing for sure—Camp Rock rocked.